THIS WALKER BOOK BELONGS TO:

_____

_____

_____

_____

To little ghouls
everywhere,
especially
Finbar and Sally

First published 1993 by
Walker Books Ltd
87 Vauxhall Walk, London SE11 5HJ

This edition published 1995

2 4 6 8 10 9 7 5 3

© 1993 Colin and Jacqui Hawkins

This book has been typeset in Bernhard.

Printed in Hong Kong

British Library Cataloguing in Publication Data
A catalogue record for this book is available
from the British Library.
ISBN 0-7445-3671-5

Come for a Ride on the
GHOST TRAIN

Colin & Jacqui Hawkins

WALKER BOOKS
AND SUBSIDIARIES
LONDON · BOSTON · SYDNEY

Come for a ride

on the Ghost Train.

In the dark dark

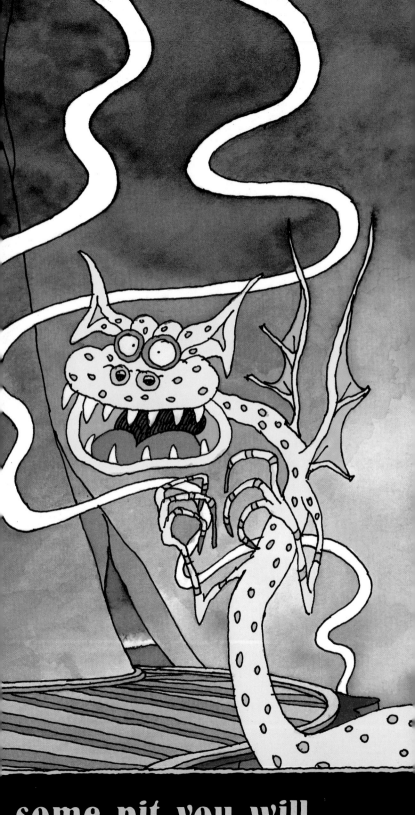

some pit you will...

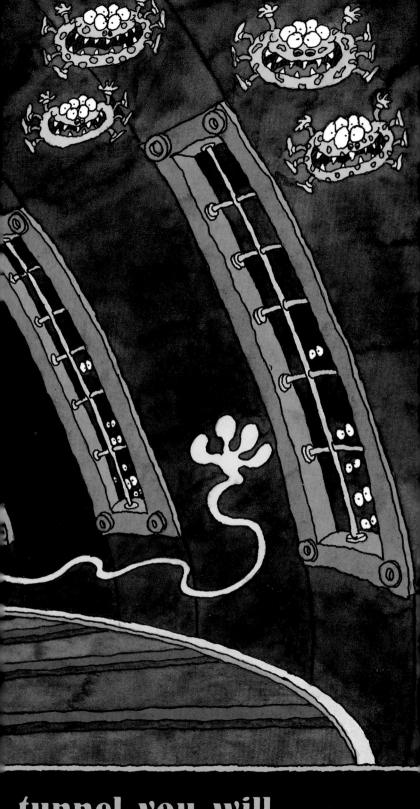

tunnel you will...

swamp you will...

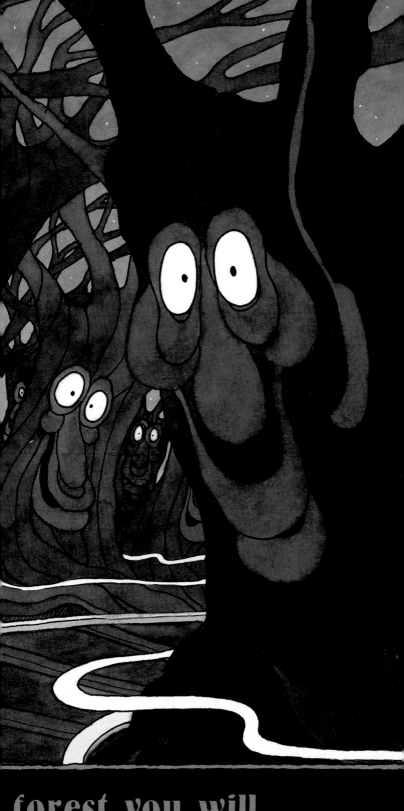

forest you will...

Deep in the scary

In the gruesome

graveyard you will...

At the haunted

chapel you will...

SSCREEECH!

In the dark dark

DEAD!

In the creepy casket, in the

crypt you will...

STOP

dark dark crypt you will find...

MORE WALKER PAPERBACKS
For You to Enjoy

Also by Colin & Jacqui Hawkins

FARMYARD SOUNDS / JUNGLE SOUNDS

"Lots of jolly cartoon-style animals… Every child I've ever known loves making animal noises, so be prepared to do your stuff." *Tony Bradman, Parents*

0-7445-1752-4   *Farmyard Sounds*   £3.99
0-7445-1753-2   *Jungle Sounds*   £3.99

TERRIBLE, TERRIBLE TIGER / THE WIZARD'S CAT

Two wonderfully entertaining rhyming picture books about a tiger who is not quite what he seems and a cat who wishes he were something else!

0-7445-1063-5   *Terrible, Terrible Tiger*   £3.99
0-7445-1389-8   *The Wizard's Cat*   £3.99

WHERE'S MY MUMMY?

Duckling is looking for his mummy. But who is it? Is it the dog, the cat or the hen?
Where is his mummy? Young children will have great fun helping duckling to bring his search to a happy conclusion.

0-7445-3041-5   £3.99

I'M NOT SLEEPY!

Baby Bear is adorable, cuddly and very naughty. At bedtime, he just won't settle down to sleep: he wants a glass of water, a biscuit, his toys… Young children will love his attempts to gain attention.

0-7445-3042-3   £3.99

Walker Paperbacks are available from most booksellers, or by post from B.B.C.S., P.O. Box 941, Hull, North Humberside HU1 3YQ

24 hour telephone credit card line 01482 224626

To order, send: Title, author, ISBN number and price for each book ordered, your full name and address,
cheque or postal order payable to BBCS for the total amount and allow the following for postage and packing:
UK and BFPO: £1.00 for the first book, and 50p for each additional book to a maximum of £3.50.
Overseas and Eire: £2.00 for the first book, £1.00 for the second and 50p for each additional book.

Prices and availability are subject to change without notice.